SUPER
SANDCASTLE
Creature Features

What Has a Shell?

Mary Elizabeth Salzmann

ABDO
Publishing Company

Published by ABDO Publishing Company, 8000 West 78th Street, Edina, Minnesota 55439. Copyright © 2008 by Abdo Consulting Group, Inc. International copyrights reserved in all countries. No part of this book may be reproduced in any form without written permission from the publisher. Super SandCastle™ is a trademark and logo of ABDO Publishing Company.

Printed in the United States.

Credits
Editor: Pam Price
Content Developer: Nancy Tuminelly
Cover and Interior Design and Production: Mighty Media
Photo Credits: iStockphoto (Nancy Kennedy, Dan Schmitt, Harry Thomas), Doug Perrine/SeaPics.com, Shutterstock, Steve Wewerka

Library of Congress Cataloging-in-Publication Data

Salzmann, Mary Elizabeth, 1968-

What has a shell? / Mary Elizabeth Salzmann.

p. cm. -- (Creature features)

ISBN 978-1-59928-871-0

1. Mollusks--Juvenile literature. 2. Crustacea--Juvenile literature. 3. Reptiles--Juvenile literature. 4. Shells--Juvenile literature. I. Title.

QL405.2.S256 2007

591.47'7--dc22

2007010188

Super SandCastle™ books are created by a team of professional educators, reading specialists, and content developers around five essential components— phonemic awareness, phonics, vocabulary, text comprehension, and fluency— to assist young readers as they develop reading skills and strategies and increase their general knowledge. All books are written, reviewed, and leveled for guided reading, early reading intervention, and Accelerated Reader® programs for use in shared, guided, and independent reading and writing activities to support a balanced approach to literacy instruction.

About SUPER SANDCASTLE™

Bigger Books for Emerging Readers
Grades PreK–3

Created for library, classroom, and at-home use, Super SandCastle™ books support and engage young readers as they develop and build literacy skills and will increase their general knowledge about the world around them. Super SandCastle™ books are part of SandCastle™, the leading PreK–3 imprint for emerging and beginning readers. Super SandCastle™ features a larger trim size for more reading fun.

Let Us Know
Super SandCastle™ would like to hear your stories about reading this book. What was your favorite page? Was there something hard that you needed help with? Share the ups and downs of learning to read. We want to hear from you! Send us an e-mail.

sandcastle@abdopublishing.com

Contact us for a complete list of SandCastle™, Super SandCastle™, and other nonfiction and fiction titles from ABDO Publishing Company.

www.abdopublishing.com • 8000 West 78th Street Edina, MN 55439 • 800-800-1312 • 952-831-1632 fax

A shell is the hard outer covering of an animal.
The shell helps protect the creature's body.

A snail has a shell.

Snails are part of a huge family of shelled creatures called mollusks. A mollusk's body releases calcium carbonate, which hardens to form its shell.

A clam has a shell.

A clam shell is divided into two halves. The shell has a hinge so it can open and close. Clams and other mollusks with hinged shells are called bivalves.

A nautilus has a shell.

The inside of a nautilus shell is divided into chambers. As the nautilus grows, more chambers are added.

A crayfish has a shell.

A crayfish shell is called an exoskeleton. As they get bigger, crayfish shed their exoskeletons and grow new ones.

A hermit crab has a shell.

Hermit crabs have exoskeletons like crayfish do. But for extra protection, they move into empty mollusk shells and carry them around.

A beetle has a shell.

A beetle's shell includes an exoskeleton and hard outer wings. When they fly, beetles raise their outer wings so the flight wings underneath can move.

A tortoise has a shell.

The top part of a tortoise shell is called the carapace. The underside is called the plastron. Tortoises can live for more than 170 years.

A sea turtle has a shell.

Sea turtle shells are very similar to the shells of land turtles and tortoises. However, a sea turtle can't retract its legs and head into its shell.

An armadillo has a shell.

The armadillo's shell is called armor. It is made of bone covered with scales. Armadillos live in warm areas in North America and South America.

What would you do if you had a shell?

MORE CREATURES
THAT HAVE SHELLS

crab

turtle

oyster

scorpion

lobster

GLOSSARY

calcium carbonate - a white, natural compound.

chamber - an enclosed space or section.

divided - separated into groups or parts.

exoskeleton - a hard outer body covering.

hinge - a joint that allows two attached parts to move.

mollusk - an animal with a soft body and a hard shell, such as a clam or a snail.

protect - to guard someone or something from harm or danger.

release - to set free or let go.

retract - to pull back in.

shed - to lose something, such as skin, leaves, or fur, through a natural process.

similar - having characteristics in common.

underneath - under or below something else.